Frog Legs

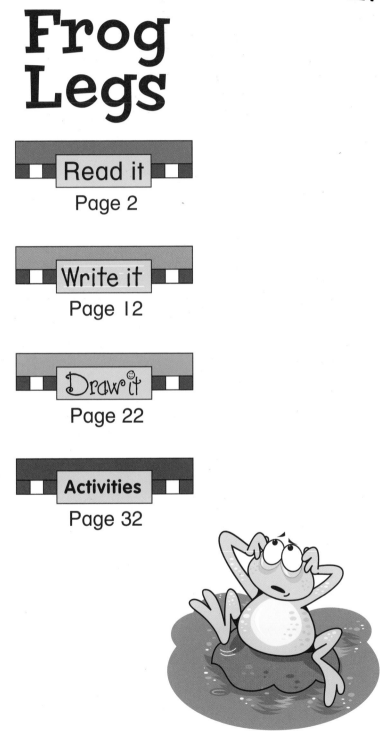

Frog was sad. He sat on a rock
and looked in the pond.

"I want to be like the other frogs.
But I cannot HOP!" said Frog.

I can jump up and do a flip.

But I still cannot HOP!

I can run down a hill and dig in the mud.

But I still cannot HOP!

I can hit a home run with a bat.

But I still *cannot* HOP!

"No one will play with a frog that *cannot* HOP!" said Frog.

Just then, the other frogs jumped
up on the rock to sit with Frog.

Read it

"Can we play with you?" asked the other frogs.

"But I cannot HOP!" said Frog.

"Yes, but you can jump, flip, run, dig, and hit with a bat! And we want to be just like *you!*"

Frog was sad.

He sat on a rock and

looked in the pond.

"I want to be like the other frogs, but I cannot HOP!" said Frog.

I can _jump_ up

and do a _flip_ .

But I still cannot

HOP !

I can run down a
__hill__ and dig in
the __mud__. But I
still cannot HOP!

I can hit a home

run with a bat.

But I still *cannot*

HOP !

"No one will play

with a frog

that *cannot* HOP!"

said Frog.

Just then, the other

frogs jumped

up on the rock

to sit with Frog.

"Can we play

with you ?"

asked the other

frogs.

"But I cannot HOP !" said Frog.

"Yes, but you can jump, flip, run, dig, and hit with a bat! And we want to be just like *you!*"

Frog was sad. He sat on a rock and looked in the pond.

"I want to be like the other frogs.
But I cannot HOP!" said Frog.

I can jump up and do a flip.

But I still cannot HOP!

I can run down a hill and dig in the mud.

But I still cannot HOP!

I can hit a home run with a bat.

But I still *cannot* HOP!"

"No one will play with a frog that *cannot* HOP!" said Frog.

Just then, the other frogs jumped
up on the rock to sit with Frog.

"Can we play with you?" asked
the other frogs.

"But I cannot hop!" said Frog.

Draw it

"Yes, but you can jump, flip, run, dig, and hit with a bat! We want to be just like *you!*"

Read it

Play bulls-eye words or letters! To help your child or student practice reading words or recognizing letters of the alphabet, write the words or letters onto index cards or small pieces of paper. Next, stick the paper onto your refrigerator or a magnetic board. Have the child throw a magnetic toy dart (or a crayon with magnetic tape adhered to its tip) at the board. Whichever letter or word the dart lands on is the one your child has to read out loud. It's active, it's fun, and, best of all, it will get your child reading.

Write it

Label your room! This is a great activity to help your child or student practice inventive spelling before beginning to spell conventionally. Start with a pencil, a stack of medium-sized sticky notes, and a room of your choosing. Select items in the room, and have the child label them with sticky notes. He or she can use inventive spelling to sound out each word as he or she writes it. You can even set a goal for the child to use a certain number of sticky notes before moving on to other rooms.

Draw it

Draw someplace new! Spice up your child or student's drawing life by using a variety of cool surfaces to draw on. Try having him or her draw on an old white t-shirt, a brown lunch bag, tracing paper, paper cut into shapes (circles, triangles, diamonds, etc.), an old cardboard box, a plastic tablecloth, or anything else you can think of!

A NOTE TO PARENTS:
When children create their own spellings for words they don't know, they are using **inventive spelling**. For the beginner, the act of writing is more important than the correctness of form. Sounding out words and predicting how they will be spelled reinforces an under-standing of the connection between letters and sounds. Eventually, through experimenting with spelling patterns and repeated exposure to standard spelling, children will learn and use the correct form in their own writing. Until then, inventive spelling encourages early experimentation and self-expression in writing and nurtures a child's confidence as a writer.